Genetic Diseases and Disorders™

Alopecia Areata

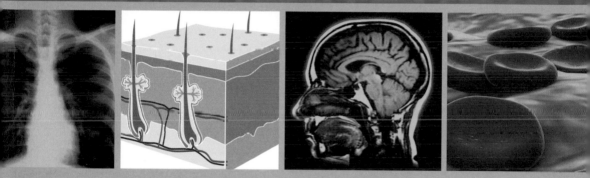

Janey Levy

The Rosen Publishing Group, Inc., New York

Published in 2007 by The Rosen Publishing Group, Inc.
29 East 21st Street, New York, NY 10010

First Edition

Library of Congress Cataloging-in-Publication Data

Alopecia areata / Janey Levy.
    p. cm.—(Genetic diseases and disorders)
Includes bibliographical references and index.
ISBN 1-4042-0693-0 (library binding)
1. Alopecia areata—Juvenile literature.
I. Title. II. Series.
RL155.5.L48 2005
616.5'46—dc22

2005033232

Manufactured in the United States of America

On the cover: Background: cross-section of the human scalp. Foreground: cross-section of skin showing hair follicles.

Contents

Introduction

Alopecia areata is a disease that causes sudden hair loss, usually in round patches. The name, which is Latin, describes the disease. *Alopecia* means "hair loss," or "baldness." *Areata* means "occurring in patches." The disease usually affects the scalp but can affect the rest of the body as well.

Most scientists believe alopecia areata is an autoimmune disease. The immune system protects the body from disease by attacking and destroying germs and other invaders. Sometimes, however, it mistakenly attacks the body itself, causing an autoimmune disease. In alopecia areata, the immune system attacks groups of hair follicles, the tiny, cup-shaped structures from which hair grows. The follicles shrink and quit growing hair, resulting in bald patches.

Alopecia areata usually begins as a few small bald patches that appear suddenly on the scalp. The bare skin in the patches looks smooth and normal. Usually, no other symptoms accompany the bald patches. Occasionally,

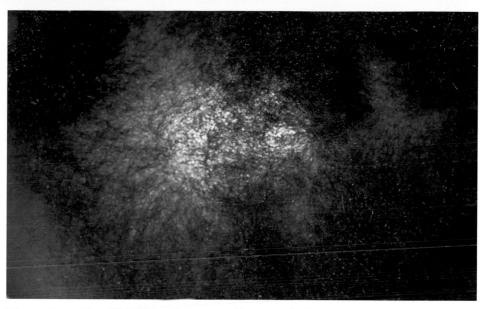

There is no "normal" or "average" case of alopecia areata. However, when the disease does strike, the scalp *(above)* is usually the first site on the body to lose hair. The first hair loss often occurs very suddenly, so the onset of the disease can leave a person confused, embarrassed, or angry.

however, there is a burning sensation or mild itching, tingling, or tenderness.

The disease's progress varies from person to person, and there is no way to predict what will happen. Some people develop only a few bald patches, regrow their hair within about a year, and never lose hair again. Other people develop many bald patches and lose hair and regrow it over and over again for many years. People with alopecia totalis lose all their scalp hair. People with alopecia universalis lose all the hair on their whole body, including eyebrows, eyelashes, and ear and nose hair.

Alopecia areata does not cause physical pain and cannot kill a person. However, it can cause great emotional stress because of its effects on a person's appearance. People with alopecia universalis may suffer more allergies and illnesses because more dust and germs can enter their eyes, nose, and ears.

Alopecia areata can strike anyone. About five million people in the United States have the disease. Most people with the disease experience their first episode of hair loss before the age of twenty. However, about 40 percent suffer their first episode as fully grown adults.

About one out of every five people with alopecia areata has a family member with the disease. In addition, people with alopecia areata are likely to have family members who suffer from other autoimmune diseases, such as type 1 diabetes, rheumatoid arthritis, lupus, thyroid disease, pernicious anemia, and inflammatory bowel syndrome. People who have alopecia areata are also more susceptible to respiratory problems such as asthma and skin conditions such as atopic dermatitis (eczema).

Scientists believe that more than one gene is involved in alopecia areata. When these genes are present together, they make a person susceptible to the disease. However, just having the genes does not mean a person will develop alopecia areata. Some other factors trigger the immune system to attack hair follicles. Different factors may trigger the disease in different people. These factors could be viruses, something in the environment, or even something in a person's body.

Today, scientists are trying to identify the genes involved in alopecia areata in order to learn how they interact. Scientists are also working to identify the triggering factors. They hope the research will lead to new and more effective treatments for this emotionally painful disease.

Two Thousand Years of Alopecia Areata

1

The earliest references to alopecia appear in ancient Greek and Roman writings. Around 400 BC, the Greek physician Hippocrates (circa 460 BC–377 BC) first used the Greek term *alopekia*, from which the Latin term *alopecia* comes. However, he probably was not describing the disease we know today as alopecia areata. *Alōpekia* literally means "fox's disease." Hippocrates may have been referring to mange, a disease that is common in foxes. It also occurs in other mammals, including humans. Like alopecia areata, mange causes patchy hair loss. In mange, however, the skin in the bald patches is not smooth and normal. It is red, puffy, and very itchy. Mange is caused by mites, tiny animals that are related to spiders.

More than four centuries after Hippocrates, a Roman writer named Aulus Cornelius Celsus

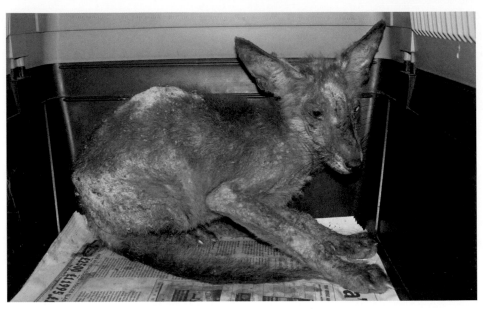

The word *alopecia* comes from the Greek *alōpekia* (literally, "fox's disease"). *Alōpekia* probably described mange, the condition afflicting the fox seen here. *Alōpekia* entered Latin as *alopecia*, which became the general medical term for hair loss in both animals and humans.

gave the first description of what is clearly the disease we know as alopecia areata. Celsus described two forms of alopecia in a medical encyclopedia titled *De Medicina* that he wrote around AD 30. One form was complete baldness that occurred in people of all ages. The second was a winding pattern of bald patches across the scalp. Celsus called this form *ophiasis*, which means "snake," because the winding pattern reminded him of a snake. He incorrectly wrote that *ophiasis* occurred only in children.

Alopecia Areata Gets Its Name

The name "alopecia areata" was not used until many centuries after Hippocrates and Celsus. The first person to use it was a

THE FATHER OF MODERN MEDICINE

Hippocrates, shown here, was considered the greatest physician of his time. Today he is thought of as the father of modern medicine. Hippocrates rejected the idea that illness resulted from evil spirits or punishment by the gods. He believed that illness had a physical cause, and he based his practice of medicine on the study of the human body. He is also credited with developing the oath of medical ethics that is still taken by physicians today. Hippocrates himself was bald and tried many ways to regrow his hair. One of the remedies he tried was a mixture of horseradish, pigeon droppings, beetroot, and other ingredients that he spread on his head. It didn't work.

French physician named François Boissier de Sauvages de la Croix. It appeared in a book he published in 1763 titled *Nosologia Methodica*. This book was an early attempt to classify diseases, or organize them into groups. Many others like it followed. Since little was known about the causes of diseases, these books grouped diseases according to their symptoms.

Nineteenth-Century Ideas About the Cause

As medical knowledge grew, physicians attempted to identify the cause of alopecia areata. By the late 1800s, two main

TCGATTCTGAACATGATACGTACTGGTCCACTAGAACTGAACTCGAGAGGTACTAG

DESPERATE MEASURES

Over the centuries, people have tried many different remedies for baldness, all unsuccessful. These include:

◀ Spider webs
◀ Dog urine
◀ Oil of wormwood
◀ German army horse salve
◀ Equal parts of Abyssinian greyhound's heel, date blossoms, and ass's hoof, boiled together in oil
◀ Equal parts of fat of a lion, a hippopotamus, a crocodile, a goose, a snake, and a wild goat known as an ibex
◀ A mixture of horseradish, mustard oil, citrus peel, and egg yolk
◀ Dew collected from the traditional healing plant known as Saint-John's-wort
◀ A mixture of burned domestic mice, horse teeth, bear grease, and bone marrow from deer

hypotheses had emerged. One was that an infection caused by parasites produced the disease. The other was that a nerve-related disorder caused it.

Physicians who believed the parasite hypothesis pointed out that the area of hair loss slowly expanded in size. This is exactly what would happen if there were an infection at the site of hair loss. Physicians also noticed that institutions like schools and orphanages often seemed to have large numbers of cases of alopecia areata. This was what would be expected if there were an infection that was spreading from person to person. Discoveries that parasites caused other diseases, such as ringworm, made the parasite hypothesis for alopecia areata seem like a good explanation. Nevertheless, physicians were unable to identify a specific parasite that might cause alopecia areata.

Other physicians supported the idea that a nerve-related disorder caused alopecia areata. This hypothesis was known as the trophoneurotic, neurotrophic, or neuropathic hypothesis. All these names refer to nerves that do not function properly. The cause of the problem was thought to be emotional stress or physical damage to the nerves, which harmed hair follicles. Most dermatologists, or skin doctors, came to believe that a nervous disorder was probably the cause of alopecia areata. In support of this hypothesis, they pointed to the fact that people who had recently developed alopecia areata frequently displayed emotional stress. However, it often was unclear if stress was caused by the hair loss or the other way around.

Twentieth-Century Ideas About the Cause

In the early twentieth century, physicians proposed some unusual variations on the nerve-related hypothesis. For instance, in 1902, a French dermatologist named Leonard Jacquet suggested that diseased teeth caused nerve irritation, which led to alopecia areata. This was disproved in 1910, when another physician showed that people without alopecia areata were just as likely to have diseased teeth. Another variation on the nerve-related hypothesis appeared in 1939, when a Scottish physician proposed that eyestrain caused alopecia areata. This idea did not win wide acceptance.

New theories about the cause of alopecia areata appeared in the early twentieth century. In 1912, a British doctor named Horatio George Adamson (1860–1955) suggested that poison carried to hair follicles by the bloodstream caused hair loss. Adamson and others thought this hypothesis provided a good explanation for why hair loss occurred at many places on the body at the same time. An experiment seemed to provide some support for Adamson's hypothesis. Among people who were given small amounts of rat poison, some developed patchy hair loss similar to alopecia areata. However, in spite of this evidence, few physicians believed that poison caused alopecia areata.

Another theory proposed in the early twentieth century was the endocrine hypothesis. This hypothesis was based on the fact that people with alopecia areata were much more likely than other people to have disorders of endocrine glands, especially the thyroid. This gland, located in the neck, produces crucial hormones. These hormones regulate important processes in the body, including the growth rate of children.

By the 1920s, most dermatologists had come to the conclusion that either the nerve-related or the endocrine hypothesis offered the best explanation for the cause of alopecia areata. Yet it was research done long before the 1920s that would eventually lead to a new understanding of alopecia areata. Back in 1891, a study published in a French journal had shown that cells from the immune system invaded hair follicles affected by alopecia areata. This was the first hint that alopecia areata might be an autoimmune disease. However, no one at the time could have recognized that. In 1891, the concept of autoimmune disease did not exist. It was not until the 1950s and 1960s that most physicians came to accept the idea of autoimmune diseases. And it was only in the 1980s that many physicians and scientists began to think that alopecia areata might be an autoimmune disease.

Current Ideas About the Cause

Today, most physicians and scientists believe the autoimmune hypothesis. They think that a person's immune system mistakes

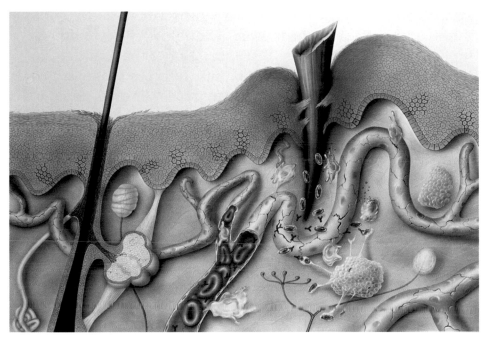

With alopecia areata, a person's immune system treats hair follicles in much the same way it treats foreign invaders like bacteria. This illustration shows the immune system responding to a thorn that has pierced the skin, bringing bacteria with it. The immune system identifies the bacteria as harmful and responds with white blood cells (the pale blue shapes above). These cells seek out and destroy the bacteria to remove the danger. The thin, dark figure at right is a hair shaft protruding up through the skin.

hair follicles for dangerous invaders and attacks them, causing hair loss. They point to four pieces of evidence that support this hypothesis. First, some people with alopecia areata regrow hair when they are given drugs that are meant to affect the immune system. This suggests that the immune system is somehow involved in alopecia areata. Second, some people with alopecia areata have more antibodies in their

GATTCTGAACATGATACGTACTGGTCCACTAGAACTGAACTCGAGAGGTACTAGA

blood than normal. Antibodies are substances that are produced by the immune system when it is trying to defend the body against invaders. Third, cells from the immune system that are not usually found in hair follicles *are* found in the follicles of people with alopecia areata. Fourth, people with alopecia areata are more likely than other people to have another autoimmune disease or to have a family member with an autoimmune disease.

Autoimmune diseases raise certain questions. Why do some people get them and others do not? Why do autoimmune diseases often run in families? In the 1970s, physicians and scientists began to suspect that genetic factors were involved. Research to identify the gene or genes that might be involved in alopecia areata began in the 1980s. This research is still being carried out today. Studies have shown that alopecia areata is probably a polygenic disease, which means that there are many genes involved. Physicians and scientists do not believe that everyone who has these genes will develop the disease. However, they believe that an individual who does have these genes is more susceptible to developing the disease. Some other factor—a virus, something in the environment, or something in a person's body—can trigger the disease in someone who possesses the genes.

The fact that alopecia areata is a polygenic disease rather than a disease caused by a single gene has a great effect on efforts to study and treat it. Polygenic diseases require many more years of research to identify all the genes involved and find out how they work together. In fact, it wasn't until the late twentieth century that physicians and scientists gained the knowledge they needed to study the genetics of a complex polygenic disease like alopecia areata. It took about a century of genetic research to reach that point.

2

Genes are the basic units of heredity. Every living cell contains genes. They are found on structures called chromosomes, which are made of proteins and deoxyribonucleic acid, or DNA. An organism's complete set of DNA is known as its genome. Individual genes are stretches of the genome's DNA that tell the cell how to make the proteins necessary for life. Genes make up only part of the genome. The rest of the DNA in the genome performs functions not involved with heredity.

Different living things have different numbers of genes and chromosomes. It is thought that humans have approximately 25,000 genes, which are arranged on twenty-three pairs of chromosomes. Each person inherits one set of twenty-three chromosomes from his or her

CGATTCTGAACATGATACGTACTGGTCCACTAGAACTGAACTCGAGAGGTACTAGA

mother and one set from his or her father. The genes on these chromosomes determine such things as what color hair and eyes the person will have and how tall the person will be. They also determine whether the person will have a genetic disease (or be susceptible to developing one). Physicians and scientists know all these things now, but for most of human history, heredity was a great mystery. Most of what is known about genetics has been learned in the last century or so.

Early Genetic Research

The story actually starts in the second half of the 1800s, when improved microscopes led to the discovery of chromosomes in cells. Before then, scientists did not know such structures existed. By the late 1800s, studies of cells and cell reproduction had led some scientists to believe that chromosomes were the basis of heredity. However, that idea was not widely accepted. Then, in 1909, Thomas Hunt Morgan and a team of scientists began studying genetics using fruit flies. The men wanted to study the inheritance of traits over several generations, and fruit flies were the perfect subjects to study. They mature and reproduce quickly, giving scientists several generations to study in just a short time. Morgan and his team studied the inheritance of traits such as eye color and wing shape. Their work provided the first proof that genes are the units of heredity. It also showed that genes are located on chromosomes.

Mutations, or genetic changes, often appeared in Morgan's fruit flies. By studying these mutations, Morgan and his team were able to determine what traits each gene affected. They were also able to determine where each gene was located. In other words, they made the first genetic map.

Even with the discoveries made by Morgan and his team, little was known about the function and structure of genes

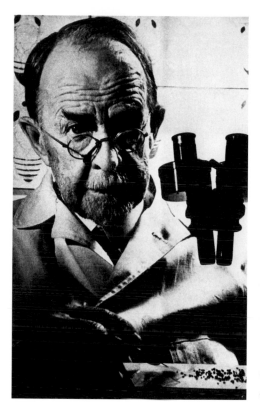

American scientist Thomas Hunt Morgan received many honors for his work in genetics. He was made a foreign member of the Royal Society of London in 1919. The society awarded Morgan its Darwin Medal in 1924 and its Copley Medal in 1939. In between these awards, in 1933, Morgan received the Nobel Prize in Physiology or Medicine for discoveries in genetics.

and chromosomes. Important advances were made in the 1940s. Early in that decade, George W. Beadle and Edward L. Tatum carried out genetic experiments with a fungus. They discovered that genes control chemical reactions in cells by directing the production of special proteins called enzymes. The two men also determined that there is one specific gene for each enzyme. Beadle and Tatum's work provided important information about how genes work. However, it still was not clear which part of the material found in chromosomes made up the genes.

DNA

Scientists had known for a long time that chromosomes were made up of DNA and proteins. In 1869, Johann Friedrich Miescher discovered DNA, which he called nuclein, during

TCGATTCTGAACATGATACGTACTGGTCCACTAGAACTGAACTCGAGAGGTACTAG

his studies of white blood cells. At the time, however, no one thought this discovery was very important. Proteins are essential to life processes, and most scientists believed that the proteins in chromosomes were the basis of heredity. Then, in 1944, a team of scientists led by Oswald T. Avery carried out

THE DNA LADDER

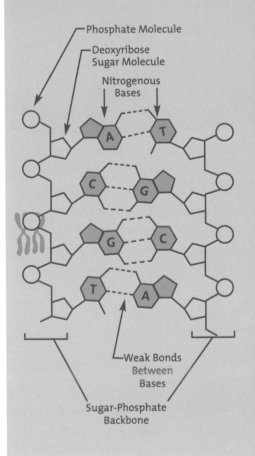

Phosphate Molecule

Deoxyribose Sugar Molecule

Nitrogenous Bases

Weak Bonds Between Bases

Sugar-Phosphate Backbone

DNA consists of chemical building blocks called nucleotides. Each nucleotide has three parts: a compound called a phosphate, a sugar called deoxyribose, and a nitrogenous compound called a base. All nucleotides have the same phosphate and sugar. There are four different bases: adenine (A), guanine (G), thymine (T), and cytosine (C). When these building blocks join together in DNA, the phosphates and sugars form the sides of the ladder. The bases, which are connected by weak chemical bonds, form the rungs. The sequence of nucleotides in the DNA determines the genetic code.

Oswald T. Avery and his team published their DNA research in the *Journal of Experimental Medicine* in 1944. At first, not all scientists accepted the conclusions of Avery's team. But experiments conducted by other scientists in the early 1950s proved that Avery and his team were correct.

experiments on DNA from bacteria. Their work showed that DNA alone determines heredity. Following this discovery, scientists began to focus research on learning more about DNA.

Scientists knew that DNA was composed of chemical building blocks called nucleotides. There are four different nucleotides: A, G, T, and C. But scientists didn't know how the nucleotides fit together to form DNA. Knowing the structure of DNA would be important for understanding how it worked. Finally, in 1953, James Watson and Francis Crick proposed that the structure of DNA was a double helix, which resembles a ladder twisted into a spiral. Research carried out since 1953 has shown that they were correct.

The Genetic Code

The nucleotides in DNA are arranged in groups of three called codons. Each codon instructs the cell to make an amino acid.

TCGATTCTGAACATGATACGTACTGGTCCACTAGAACTGAACTCGAGAGGTACTA

A young Marshall W. Nirenberg is shown here in his office at the National Institutes of Health. Nirenberg began research into DNA and the production of proteins in 1959. These early experiments formed the foundation of his work on the genetic code in the early 1960s. In 1962, the National Academy of Sciences honored Nirenberg with the Molecular Biology Award.

A series of amino acids makes up a protein. After the work of Watson and Crick, the next big challenge in genetics research was learning to read this code, or determining which codon corresponds to each amino acid.

In 1962, Marshall W. Nirenberg discovered the genetic code for one amino acid. In following years, Nirenberg and other scientists determined the codes for all twenty amino acids used to build proteins in humans. Being able to read a gene's code meant scientists could begin to understand the gene's function. It also meant they could recognize when there was a mutation in the gene.

Genetic Research in the Late Twentieth Century

Researchers developed new methods for studying genes in the 1970s. They discovered how to remove genes from one organism and insert them into another organism. Because this technique recombines DNA from one organism with DNA from another, it is known as recombinant DNA technology. Experiments with recombinant DNA technology have helped scientists learn more about both the structure and function of genes.

As a result of the research done over the course of the twentieth century, physicians and scientists knew quite a bit about genes by the 1980s. This knowledge provided a starting point for researchers who wanted to study genetic diseases. But much of this knowledge came from research carried out on organisms other than humans. Therefore, the information scientists gathered about genes and heredity had to do with general principles that apply to the genes of all living things. Much was still unknown about the specific genes that humans have. Gaining that knowledge became the next big goal in genetics research.

The Human Genome Project

In 1990, the U.S. National Institutes of Health (NIH) and the U.S. Department of Energy (DOE) jointly launched the

TCGATTCTGAACATGATACGTACTGGTCCACTAGAACTGAACTCGAGAGGTACTAC

This researcher is injecting DNA strands into a thin layer of gel
between two pieces of glass. The gel plate will be placed in a machine
known as a sequencer, which analyzes the nucleotide sequence. In
the late 1970s, a skilled researcher working by hand could determine
the sequence of about 5,000 bases in a week. Today's automated
sequencers can read more than 400,000 bases in a single day.

Human Genome Project. Aided by international organizations,
the NIH and DOE began the task of determining the sequence
of the nucleotides in human DNA and identifying all the
genes in the human genome. This was an enormous under-
taking. (The human body contains billions of miles of
DNA!) In spite of the challenges, researchers working on the
project were able to meet their goals ahead of schedule. By
2003, they had established the sequence of nucleotides in
the entire human genome. By April 2005, researchers had

SOME THINGS WE'VE LEARNED

Results of the Human Genome Project have made it clear that there is still much to learn about genetics. Below are some of the things discovered so far.

◄ The human genome contains about three billion nucleotides.
◄ The average gene contains 3,000 nucleotides.
◄ The largest gene, known as dystrophin, is responsible for the production of a muscle protein and contains 2.4 million nucleotides.
◄ The functions of more than half of the genes in the human genome are unknown.
◄ The number of genes on a chromosome ranges from 231 to 2,968.

mapped the locations of the genes on about two-thirds of the forty-six human chromosomes.

Scientists are eagerly using information gained from the Human Genome Project. They apply their knowledge to carry out new research into genetic diseases, with the goal of finding better treatments or even cures for the diseases. Having the complete sequence of human DNA is especially critical for the study of polygenic diseases such as alopecia areata, which may involve many genes located on different chromosomes. The research currently underway offers new hope to people with alopecia areata. Perhaps scientists will soon gain a better understanding of the disease, learn why certain people get it, and begin to treat it more effectively.

Who Gets Alopecia Areata, and What Can You Do About It?

3

Scientists hope one day to have a genetic test that will identify people who are susceptible to developing alopecia areata. Currently, physicians can run genetic tests for such diseases as breast and colon cancer. Until similar tests are designed for alopecia areata, there is no clear way to predict who will develop the disease. It strikes people of all races and ethnic backgrounds, it affects males and females equally, and it can strike at any age. About 60 percent of people with alopecia areata experience their first episode of hair loss before they are twenty years old. There have even been reports of babies born with alopecia areata. In the United States alone, nearly five million people have experienced episodes of hair loss caused by alopecia areata.

Risk Factors

About 20 percent of people with alopecia areata have a family member with the disease. If you have a close family member with alopecia areata, you have a slightly greater chance of developing it. If that family member experienced the first episode of hair loss before thirty years of age, your risk is further increased.

Having a family member with another autoimmune disease also increases the chances that you will develop alopecia areata. Scientists have identified many autoimmune diseases that seem to occur more often than usual among the family members of people with alopecia areata. These diseases include type 1 diabetes, rheumatoid arthritis, lupus, thyroid disease, pernicious anemia, inflammatory bowel disease, Addison's disease, and vitiligo, a condition in which spots of skin permanently lose their color. In some cases, people with alopecia areata also have one of these other autoimmune diseases. Alopecia sufferers also seem to be more likely than other people to have atopy. Atopy is a genetic tendency to develop an allergic reaction such as asthma, nasal allergies, or eczema.

The Role of Genes

Researchers have identified several genes that play a role in the functioning of the immune system and seem to be involved in alopecia areata. They believe there are many more genes yet to be identified, and some of these may code for factors outside the immune system. Researchers believe that different genes play different roles in alopecia areata. Some genes make a person susceptible to developing the disease, while others affect how severe it will be, how long it will last, and how well it will respond to treatment. Having the alopecia areata genes

TCGATTCTGAACATGATACGTACTGGTCCACTAGAACTGAACTCGAGAGGTACTAC

does not mean that a person will definitely develop the disease. Some other factor must trigger the disease, and different factors may trigger the disease for different people.

Triggers

Researchers have not yet identified the triggers for alopecia areata, but several possible triggers have been proposed. One of these is stress, which should sound familiar because it was among the possible causes of alopecia areata proposed in the 1800s. However, the theory in the 1800s was that stress directly caused alopecia areata. The modern theory, on the other hand, is that stress triggers an immune response that leads to the autoimmune disease.

Other possible triggers include physical injury, infection caused by a virus or bacteria, and allergies. These are all things that can prompt a response from the immune system. Some researchers have also proposed that exposure to certain chemicals can trigger alopecia areata. An outbreak of alopecia areata among workers at a paper factory led some scientists to suggest that long-term exposure to one of the chemicals used there had triggered the disease. Scientists also have proposed that powerful medicines used to treat other diseases may trigger alopecia areata. However, at this time, it is not yet possible to draw clear conclusions about triggers. In fact, most patients report no triggering factor preceding an episode of hair loss.

Symptoms and Progress of Alopecia Areata

Symptoms of the disease vary greatly. Some people have only one or a small number of bald patches on the scalp or

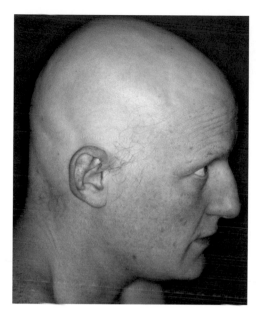

One glance tells you that this man is completely bald. Look closely and you realize his hair loss is even more extensive. He lacks eyebrows and eyelashes, and he does not have any ear hair. He has alopecia universalis, the rarest and most severe form of alopecia areata. Less than 1 percent of the people who have alopecia areata will develop this form of the disease.

elsewhere on the body. Others may have numerous bald patches. Still others may suffer alopecia totalis, the complete loss of scalp hair. In alopecia universalis, the most severe form of the disease, people lose all hair from their scalp, face, and body. Fingernails and toenails may also be affected, developing dents or grooves, or becoming misshapen. Sometimes nails even fall out.

The course of alopecia areata is unpredictable. Some people experience an episode of patchy hair loss followed by regrowth and never experience hair loss again. Others experience recurring episodes of hair loss and regrowth over many years. For a small number of people, the disease progresses to alopecia totalis or alopecia universalis.

People who have patchy hair loss on just a small area of the scalp usually experience regrowth in about a year, with or without treatment. Those with widespread hair loss are more likely to experience recurring episodes. People who have extensive hair loss and experienced their first episode before

CGATTCTGAACATGATACGTACTGGTCCACTAGAACTGAACTCGAGAGGTACTAG

Alopecia areata affects the scalp in more than two-thirds of cases. When hair loss occurs in scattered patches on the scalp, as shown at left, it is called patchy alopecia areata. Spontaneous regrowth of hair is likely in cases like the one shown, where less than 50 percent of scalp hair is lost.

they were five years old are less likely to have spontaneous regrowth or to respond well to treatment. The same is true of people whose nails are affected or who have atopy. If patchy hair loss is going to progress to alopecia totalis, it usually does so within about four months after the first hair loss. Researchers believe that people who have alopecia totalis or alopecia universalis for longer than two years are much less likely to experience spontaneous regrowth of hair. They are also less likely to respond well to treatment. However, even in cases of alopecia universalis that have lasted several years, spontaneous regrowth can occur.

Common Treatments

Several treatments are currently available, though they do not work equally well for everyone. These treatments are intended to promote new hair growth. They will not cure alopecia

THE DISEASE DIDN'T STOP HIM

At first glance, the Toronto Raptors' forward Charlie Villanueva *(left)* looks much like many other basketball players. Even his bald head isn't unusual. But when you look closely, you realize it is not only Villanueva's scalp that is missing hair. Villanueva does not have eyebrows, either. In fact, he doesn't have hair anywhere. Villanueva has alopecia universalis. He experienced his first episode of hair loss when he was ten years old. He had recurring episodes of hair loss and regrowth until he was thirteen, when his hair fell out and never grew back.

The disease, however, has not stopped Villanueva from achieving success. He was a star basketball player in high school and college before joining the Raptors in the National Basketball Association. Today, Villanueva is also the spokesperson for the Charlie's Angels Alopecia Areata Awareness Project, which is sponsored by the National Alopecia Areata Foundation.

areata and will not prevent new bald patches from developing. The treatments are most effective in mild cases of the disease.

Powerful anti-inflammatory drugs called corticosteroids are often used to treat alopecia areata. These drugs work by suppressing the immune system. They are chemically similar to a hormone called cortisol that is produced in the body.

CGATTCTGAACATGATACGTACTGGTCCACTAGAACTGAACTCGAGAGGTACTAG

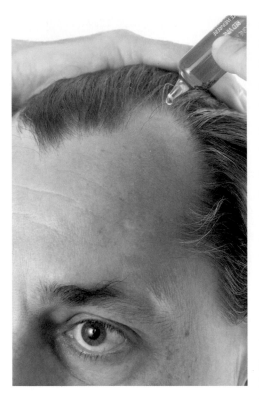

Minoxidil is used topically—meaning applied directly to the skin—to treat various forms of baldness. About 60 percent of people with common balding experience some hair regrowth with minoxidil. Up to 45 percent of people with alopecia areata experience hair regrowth. The drug is much less effective, however, for people with alopecia totalis or alopecia universalis.

Corticosteroids are taken by mouth to treat many autoimmune diseases. However, when taken this way, they can cause serious side effects, such as high blood pressure. As a result, they are not often taken by mouth to treat alopecia areata. Instead, a dermatologist uses a tiny needle to inject corticosteroids into the skin in and around the bald patches. The injections are given once a month, and if they work, new hair growth is visible in one or two months. This method is effective for most people. However, the injections can be painful, so this treatment is not recommended for children.

Topical minoxidil is safe and easy to use. Although scientists do not really understand how minoxidil works, a 5 percent topical minoxidil solution applied twice a day promotes hair regrowth. It is effective in both children and adults and can be applied to the scalp, eyebrows, and beard area. New hair growth usually appears in about twelve weeks.

Another topical treatment for alopecia areata involves anthralin cream or ointment. Anthralin, a synthetic, tarlike substance, is applied to the bald patches once a day and washed off after thirty to sixty minutes. Scientists are not sure exactly how anthralin works, but they believe it suppresses the immune system. For some people with alopecia areata, it can cause new hair growth in eight to twelve weeks. Anthralin is often used in combination with corticosteroid injections or topical minoxidil. Side effects include skin irritation and a temporary brownish stain on the treated area. Hands must always be washed after applying anthralin, and users must be careful not to get it in their eyes.

Treatments for Adults with Extensive Hair Loss

Topical immunotherapy is often used to treat adult patients with extensive hair loss. This type of treatment involves applying chemicals that cause a response from the immune system—an allergic reaction usually resulting in an itchy rash. Two chemicals commonly used for this are known as DPCP and SADBE. Scientists do not know for sure just why topical immunotherapy leads to hair regrowth. However, they think that it gets the immune system to attack the rash rather than hair follicles. About 40 percent of patients treated with topical immunotherapy experience new hair growth in three to twelve months. Topical immunotherapy is not widely used in the United States, though it is common in Canada and Europe.

Photochemotherapy, sometimes called PUVA, is another treatment used for adult patients with extensive hair loss. In this treatment, the patient is given a drug called psoralen, which causes skin to be very sensitive to ultraviolet (UV) rays.

TCGATTCTGAACATGATACGTACTGGTCCACTAGAACTGAACTCGAGAGGTACTAG

This woman's hands are being exposed to ultraviolet light to treat the skin disease known as psoriasis. Studies show that this type of treatment, called PUVA, helps most patients with psoriasis. In addition, the symptoms usually do not return for a long time following treatment. PUVA is also used to treat alopecia areata, although it is much less effective.

These are the rays that make the sun's light damaging to skin. The psoralen may be applied topically or taken by mouth. One or two hours later, the patient is exposed to an ultraviolet light source such as a tanning booth. The effectiveness of PUVA treatments is still debated, but some dermatologists have reported successful hair regrowth. However, people must receive treatments two or three times a week, and there are many drawbacks. Negative side effects of this treatment include sunburn, premature aging of skin, and the risk of developing skin cancer. Moreover, people who stop the treatments usually experience hair loss again.

Alternative Therapies

People who have unsuccessfully tried standard treatments for alopecia areata sometimes turn to what are called alternative therapies. These are ways of treating diseases that are different from the methods traditionally taught in U.S. medical schools. Often, alternative therapies come from ancient healing practices or from other cultures. They may not have been scientifically tested to determine if they work and are safe. Some may have no effect on alopecia areata, and some may actually cause more hair loss. Alternative therapies that have been used to treat hair loss include acupuncture, aromatherapy, evening primrose oil, zinc supplements, vitamins, and Chinese herbs.

When Nothing Works

Often, no treatment is effective for people with extensive hair loss. In such cases, there are other steps that can be taken to reduce the physical dangers that can result from widespread hair loss. A bald scalp needs protection from the sun, so some people choose to wear a wig, scarf, or cap. All these protect the scalp from the sun and from cold. People who do not cover their heads can use sunscreen. People who have lost eyebrows or eyelashes can wear sunglasses to protect their eyes from the sun and to help keep dirt and dust out of their eyes. Those who have lost nose hair can put ointment in their nostrils to keep germs and other organisms from entering their body through their nose.

Coping

Even when treatment helps, alopecia areata is still a difficult disease to deal with emotionally. Many people find that it is

CGATTCTGAACATGATACGTACTGGTCCACTAGAACTGAACTCGAGAGGTACTAG

NATIONAL ALOPECIA AREATA FOUNDATION

Kids Konnect — Teens — Wear With All

NAAF Home

Kids Konnect

Kids ➤

Teens ➤

Parents ➤

Disclaimer

PO Box 150760
San Rafael, CA
94915-0760

415.472.3780

Makeup and Head Covering Advice

On this Web page, you can find awesome tips from make-up pros and great head covering ideas. We'll discuss how to put on eye makeup, how to tie a scarf, and how to find wigs that fit your personality.

The National Alopecia Areata Foundation (NAAF) is dedicated to supporting those who have the disease. The Web site of the NAAF has a section called Kids Konnect, with separate pages for young children, teens, and parents. On the teen pages, visitors can find advice on topics such as makeup and head coverings. They can also read stories written by teens about what it is like to live with alopecia areata.

very helpful to share their thoughts and feelings with others who have the disease. Support groups offer one of the best ways to do this. They provide a sense of understanding and acceptance that people with alopecia areata may not find in other places. Support groups also offer an opportunity to get practical advice from people who have gone through the same thing. In addition, they may be a valuable source of information for people who need professional counseling to develop self-confidence and a positive self-image. The

National Alopecia Areata Foundation (NAAF) has support groups around the world and can help people find the nearest group. The foundation's Web site also offers a special interactive section for young people. Here, teens can give and receive advice about dealing with alopecia areata and communicate with other teens from around the world.

Current Research

4

Research into the causes and treatment of alopecia areata has dramatically increased since 1985. In that year, the National Alopecia Areata Foundation in San Rafael, California, awarded its first two research grants, each for $5,000. The foundation, which was established in 1981, is the international center for alopecia areata. It funds research, provides information to patients and their families, and organizes workshops and conferences for alopecia areata researchers and for people with the disease. Today, the NAAF is one of two major sources of funding in the United States for alopecia areata research. The other is the National Institutes of Health (NIH), a federal government agency that is devoted to medical research.

The mouse on the left is genetically normal. It has a thick, full coat of fur. The mouse on the right, however, has a gene mutation that causes alopecia areata. It shows the patchy hair loss typical of this condition. The discovery of this strain of "alopecia mouse" has greatly helped researchers studying alopecia areata in humans.

In the early years, research into alopecia areata was limited by the lack of an animal model. An animal model is an animal that exhibits a human disease. Common animal models are mice, rats, and certain monkeys. Research into the causes and possible treatments for diseases normally uses animal models. For alopecia areata, however, there was no animal model because there were no standard research animals that had the disease. Then, in 1991, scientists discovered an animal model when they found cases of alopecia areata in a particular strain of mice. This mouse model has been used extensively for alopecia areata research ever since.

TCGATTCTGAACATGATACGTACTGGTCCACTAGAACTGAACTCGAGAGGTACTA

Today, alopecia areata research focuses on both the cause and the treatment of the disease. Scientists in the United States, Canada, Australia, Europe, and Asia are carrying out a wide range of studies. This chapter highlights a sampling of current research.

The National Alopecia Areata Registry

An important step for both current and future research was taken in 2001. That year, the NIH established the National Alopecia Areata Registry. The registry is a database of information taken from thousands of people with alopecia areata and their families. In addition to written records, the registry includes blood samples—which can be used for genetic research—and digital photographs of the scalps of people with alopecia areata. All this information is available to researchers studying the genetics of alopecia areata as

DR. VERA H. PRICE, COFOUNDER OF THE NAAF

Dr. Vera H. Price, a well-known alopecia areata expert, is the cofounder of the National Alopecia Areata Foundation. She served on the foundation's board of directors from its founding in 1981 until 2003. She also serves on the NAAF's Scientific Advisory Council. Dr. Price is a physician, professor of dermatology, and researcher. In her research, she has studied how genes and the immune system relate to alopecia areata. She has also studied how hormones affect hair follicles in common balding.

well as other aspects of the disease. Information gathered from such a large and varied group of people allows researchers to carry out the kind of genetic analysis that would not be possible otherwise. The registry is located at the University of Texas M. D. Anderson Cancer Center in Houston, Texas. Other centers involved in collecting data are the University of Colorado; the University of California, San Francisco; the University of Minnesota; and Columbia University, in New York City.

Research on the Genetics of Alopecia Areata

The registry makes possible the research being carried out by Dr. Angela Christiano, a genetics professor. In 2002, using data from the registry, Dr. Christiano began the first systematic attempt to identify the genes involved in alopecia areata. Her study focuses on people with alopecia areata who come from families in which three or more individuals have the disease. Dr. Christiano is examining the entire genome of the individuals in her study to identify the genetic markers they have in common. Such a study would also not be possible without the knowledge gained from the Human Genome Project. So far, Dr. Christiano has identified areas on two chromosomes that seem to contain genes related to alopecia areata.

Another scientist studying the genetics of alopecia areata is Dr. John P. Sundberg. Dr. Sundberg, who discovered the mouse model for alopecia areata in 1991, uses mice in his research at the Jackson Laboratory in Bar Harbor, Maine. So far, his studies of mice with alopecia areata have produced detailed information regarding the areas of the mouse genome associated with the disease. His work may lead to more effective treatment in humans.

CGATTCTGAACATGATACGTACTGGTCCACTAGAACTGAACTCGAGAGGTACTAG

DR. ANGELA CHRISTIANO, GENETICS EXPERT

Dr. Angela Christiano *(below)* is one of the leading researchers in the genetics of alopecia areata. Her discovery of areas on two chromosomes that are linked to alopecia areata generated great excitement. This marked the first significant evidence of genetic susceptibility for alopecia areata that had been identified as the result of a whole genome analysis. Even before this, Dr. Christiano had made important discoveries about the genetics of alopecia. In 1997, for example, she identified a gene—known as the human hairless gene—that seems to be directly responsible for a rare genetic alopecia-type disease.

Dr. Christiano herself has alopecia areata. Her first episode of hair loss occurred just after she turned thirty, when she was going through a very stressful period in her life. She had just moved to a new city to begin an important new job. Her experience with alopecia areata led her to begin researching the disease.

Research on the Immune System's Role

Other alopecia areata researchers are studying the role of the immune system. Some scientists suspect that certain cells in hair follicles produce proteins that cause the immune system to attack the follicles, resulting in alopecia areata. Dr. John Dutz, of the University of British Columbia in Vancouver, Canada, has conducted research to try to determine which parts of the proteins are responsible. The goal is to help scientists understand how the disease develops.

Dr. Kevin McElwee, another scientist at the University of British Columbia, has conducted research into one theory about the immune system's role in alopecia areata. For the immune system to function properly, it has to be able to distinguish between normal parts of a person's body and invaders that could be dangerous. To do this, the immune system recognizes structures called antigens. Every organism, including humans, has its own distinct antigens. The immune system does not attack things in a person's body that have antigens that identify them as "self." There are also some parts of the body that are protected from attack because the immune system simply doesn't "see" them. The immune system cannot read the antigens on these parts of the body, so it ignores them. Scientists describe these areas as having an immune privilege. Hair follicles have this special protection. But if a change causes the immune system to suddenly see the hair follicles, it does not recognize them as "self" because it has never seen their antigens before. So the immune system attacks them. Dr. McElwee is examining normal hair follicles and follicles affected by alopecia areata to learn about the basic processes involved in immune privilege.

Dr. Amos Gilhar, of the Skin Research Laboratory in Haifa, Israel, is also doing research involving the loss of immune

CGATTCTGAACATGATACGTACTGGTCCACTAGAACTGAACTCGAGAGGTACTAG

privilege in hair follicles. He has caused alopecia areata to develop in mice by injecting the mice with a cytokine known as interferon gamma. Cytokines are chemical messengers that play a role in regulating the body's immune response. Interferon gamma produces alopecia areata by causing the hair follicles to be seen by the immune system. The goal of Dr. Gilhar's research is to learn more about how alopecia areata starts.

Research on Treatments

Other physicians and scientists are carrying out research into a range of treatments for alopecia areata. One treatment involves giving patients anti-interferon-gamma antibodies. A recent study showed that this may be a promising treatment for people with severe forms of alopecia areata. More research is needed to confirm the results of this study.

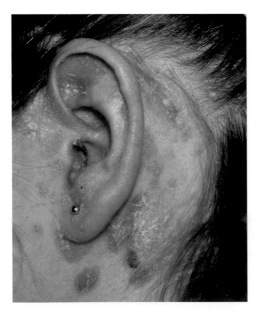

Normally, it takes skin cells about a month to mature and move from inside the skin to the surface. With psoriasis, however, this process can take only three to four days. This causes the cells to pile up on the surface and form the painful red patches seen here around this woman's ear.

Research is also being conducted to see if several drugs normally used to treat psoriasis may be effective in treating alopecia areata. Psoriasis is a skin disease that causes itchy, red patches to develop. Like alopecia areata, it is thought to be an autoimmune disease. In fact, research has shown that the two diseases have some genes in common. The psoriasis drugs currently being tested for treating alopecia areata include alefacept, efalizumab, and etanercept. Researchers hope to know soon if any of these drugs will be helpful in treating alopecia areata.

What Does the Future Hold?

5

What comes next in alopecia areata research? Many scientists agree that for the next several years, researchers will continue to do the kinds of research being done now. Research into the causes of alopecia areata will be particularly important. The hope is that a thorough understanding of the disease will lead to a cure or at least to more effective treatments than those currently available. Researchers will also continue to test possible new treatments for alopecia areata. This chapter highlights some specific avenues of future research that scientists have identified.

In regards to the treatment of alopecia areata, there are two avenues of research. One is the testing of new treatments. Scientists will be testing treatments originally developed to treat other autoimmune diseases to see if they

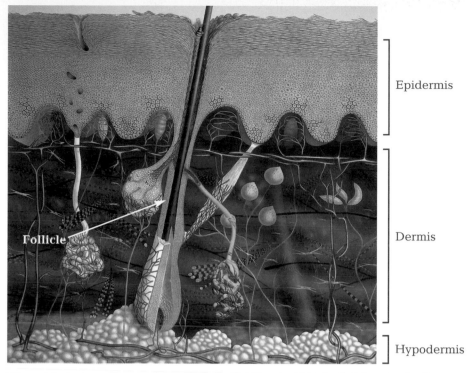

Epidermis

Dermis

Hypodermis

Follicle

The skin's top layer, the epidermis, keeps harmful bacteria from entering the body. The middle layer, the dermis, contains blood vessels, nerve endings, and oil and sweat glands. The bottom layer, the hypodermis, contains blood vessels and cells that store fat. Hair follicles extend down through the dermis to the hypodermis.

are effective in treating alopecia areata. Researchers are also developing studies to test possible treatments that work by blocking the immune response that causes alopecia areata. Some of this research will involve cytokines. As mentioned, interferon gamma is a cytokine that causes the hair follicle to be seen by the immune system and can cause alopecia areata. But researchers think they may be able to use other cytokines to slow or stop the immune system's attack on hair follicles.

Scientists will also be trying to find better ways to administer topical treatments for alopecia areata. Using current methods, not all of the medicine applied to the skin of the affected area reaches the hair follicles. Scientists hope to find a substance that will penetrate the fat under the skin to deliver the medicine directly to the hair follicles. Research has already shown that tiny

CGATTCTGAACATGATACGTACTGGTCCACTAGAACTGAACTCGAGAGGTACTAGA

synthetic spheres called liposomes do this in research animals. Now scientists need to find out if liposomes will work in people.

Searching for New Animal Models

Other scientists hope to advance alopecia areata research by identifying additional animal models. The current mouse model has the form of alopecia areata that first appears after the animal becomes an adult. Some scientists would like to have mouse models that exhibit other forms of the disease. In addition, they feel it would be useful to have models that exhibit some of the other problems sometimes found in humans with alopecia areata, such as thyroid disease and nail problems.

Some researchers also want to find other groups of animals to study. The mice with alopecia areata are not ordinary mice. They are animals that have been specially bred to show health problems so they can be used in research. Some researchers believe it would also be useful to study ordinary animals that develop the disease. Scientists have found that dogs develop alopecia areata and that the disease behaves in dogs much the same way it behaves in people. They suggest that further study of dogs with alopecia areata could improve our understanding of the disease.

Many people, however, challenge the ethics, or moral rightness, of using animals for research. They believe that lab animals suffer unnecessarily and that people don't have the right to experiment on them.

Learning More About Hair Follicles

Scientists also need to conduct research to learn more about hair follicles. Improved understanding of how follicles form, develop, and produce hair may lead to new treatments. Some researchers are beginning to study how hair follicles form in mouse embryos. Other researchers point out that much more needs to be learned about the signaling molecules in hair follicles. Signaling molecules are what the parts of the hair follicle use to "talk" to each other. Some scientists note that more needs to be learned about neurotrophins. These are proteins that, among other things, seem to be involved in regulating the resting—in contrast to the growing—phase of follicles. Still other scientists point to the need for more research into the stem cells found in follicles. Stem cells are immature cells that are responsible for new growth in the follicles. These cells appear to be uninjured in alopecia areata, and understanding them may help scientists learn more about the factors that trigger the disease.

Further Research on the Genetics of Alopecia Areata

Research into the genetics of alopecia areata is just beginning. The previous chapter discussed the current research of Dr. Angela Christiano. Her discovery of areas on two chromosomes that contain genes linked to alopecia areata is a significant first step, but it is still only a start. She hopes eventually to identify and map all the genes that play a role in alopecia areata. Similar research is also being undertaken in Europe. A group of scientists from twelve European countries is planning a study to identify the susceptibility and resistance genes in families of people with alopecia areata. Once the genes involved in the disease have been identified and mapped, scientists can begin to figure out how the genes interact with each other to cause it.

CGATTCTGAACATGATACGTACTGGTCCACTAGAACTGAACTCGAGAGGTACTAG

IS ALOPECIA AREATA NORMAL?

Dr. Kevin McElwee has suggested that the genes involved in alopecia areata are not mutations or genes that do not work properly. He thinks that they are probably normally functioning genes that, when they occur together, make a person susceptible to alopecia areata. Future research will determine whether he is right.

Gene Therapy

One possibility for the treatment of or cure for alopecia areata lies in gene therapy. Using gene therapy, scientists can alter the genes responsible for the development of some diseases. However, gene therapy for alopecia areata will not be available for many years. Scientists must first identify the genes involved in alopecia areata and understand how they interact.

Gene therapy itself must be further developed. Presently, it is still experimental. Researchers have tried gene therapy in people to treat only a few diseases. These include diseases in which the immune system does not work properly and a certain type of liver disease. In a few cases, the gene therapy worked. In other cases, it failed to correct the disease being treated or even caused other diseases. Gene therapy has also caused some deaths.

Many people believe that gene therapy offers the best hope for treating, preventing, or even curing genetic diseases for which there may be no other effective treatment. But there is considerable controversy about the ethics of gene therapy. Some people see it as "playing God" and believe

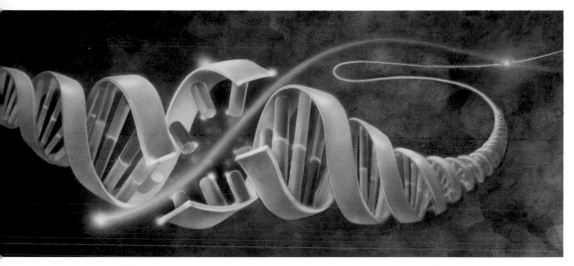

Eventually, scientists may use gene therapy to treat alopecia areata. One technique involves removing a gene that doesn't work correctly and replacing it with a normal gene. To do this, scientists must cut out the defective gene from a long strand of DNA. This cutting is done with special "chemical scissors" known as restriction enzymes. This illustration shows an artist's conception of a restriction enzyme cutting through the bonds between the bases in a strand of DNA.

that humans have neither the required knowledge nor the right to do it.

Gene therapy will not become a common treatment for anything until the difficult scientific and ethical issues surrounding it have been resolved. But perhaps sometime in the future, gene therapy will offer an effective way to treat alopecia areata.

Hope for the Future

We're standing on the threshold of a new era. Genetic breakthroughs of the past century have given scientists the tools to

CGATTCTGAACATGATACGTACTGGTCCACTAGAACTGAACTCGAGAGGTACTAG

The woman pictured here donated her hair to a charity known as Locks of Love. The charity provides hairpieces to disadvantaged young people who have lost their hair. It will take six to ten long braids like this one to make a single hairpiece. The woman understands how important a hairpiece can be to a child or a teen with hair loss—she has alopecia areata.

unlock many of the secrets of genetics, and research in the field is continuing at a rapid pace. As research into the complex genetics of alopecia areata increases our understanding of the disease, the hope grows that we will find more effective ways to treat it and perhaps even prevent or cure it.

Timeline

AD 30

Roman writer Aulus Cornelius Celsus writes the first description of what is clearly the disease we know as alopecia areata.

1763

French physician François Boissier de Sauvages de la Croix is the first person to use the term "alopecia areata."

1869

Johann Friedrich Miescher discovers DNA, but no one recognizes its importance.

Late 1800s

Two main hypotheses about the cause of alopecia areata exist: the parasite hypothesis and the nerve-related hypothesis.

1891

A study published in a French journal shows that hair follicles affected by alopecia areata have been invaded by cells from the immune system.

1909

Working with fruit flies, Thomas Hunt Morgan discovers that genes are the units of heredity. His studies lead to the first genetic map.

(continued on following page)

(continued from previous page)

1920s
Most dermatologists believe either the nerve-related or the endocrine hypothesis is the best explanation for the cause of alopecia areata.

1940s
George W. Beadle and Edward L. Tatum discover that genes control the chemical reactions in cells by directing the production of special proteins called enzymes.

1944
Oswald T. Avery shows that DNA alone, not proteins, determines heredity.

1950s
Physicians accept the idea that there are such things as autoimmune diseases.

1953
James Watson and Francis Crick propose that the structure of DNA is a double helix, like a ladder twisted into a spiral.

1962
Marshall W. Nirenberg becomes the first to crack the genetic code. He discovers the genetic code for one of the amino acids used to build proteins.

1970s
Recombinant DNA technology is developed. Scientists begin to explore the idea that genes play a role in autoimmune diseases.

1980s
Scientists begin to think that alopecia areata may be an autoimmune disease. Researchers begin to look for the genes that may be involved in alopecia areata.

1981
The National Alopecia Areata Foundation is founded.

1990

The Human Genome Project begins.

1991

John P. Sundberg discovers the mouse model for alopecia areata.

1997

Angela Christiano identifies the human hairless gene, which is believed to be responsible for a rare genetic alopecia-type disease.

2001

The National Alopecia Areata Registry is established.

2002

Angela Christiano begins the first systematic attempt to identify the genes involved in alopecia areata.

2003

Scientists involved in the Human Genome Project complete their work in determining the sequence of all the nucleotides in the human genome.

Glossary

anti-inflammatory Acting to reduce inflammation, which is the pain and swelling that may accompany injury or infection.

atopy A genetic tendency to develop an allergic reaction such as asthma, hay fever, or eczema.

autoimmune Having to do with a condition in which the immune system attacks the body itself.

disorder A physical condition that is not normal.

embryo An unborn or unhatched animal in the earliest stages of development.

endocrine Related to the system that produces hormones that are distributed in the body by the bloodstream.

heredity The passing on of characteristics from one generation to the next through genes.

hormone A chemical substance produced inside an animal that controls certain body activities.

hypothesis A tentative explanation or theory.

immunotherapy The treatment of a disease by increasing or decreasing the functioning of the immune system.

interact To act upon one another.

liposome A tiny synthetic sphere used to deliver medicine or drugs.

mutation A change in a gene. Also, the physical trait that results from such a change.

parasite An organism that lives on or in another organism. Parasites get benefits from the host organism but cause harm to it.

polygenic Involving more than one gene.

spontaneous Happening without any apparent outside influence.

stem cell A cell that has the ability to develop into any specialized cell, such as the different types of cells found in a hair follicle.

susceptible Likely to be affected by something.

symptom Evidence of a disease.

topical Applied to the surface of the body.

ultraviolet Light that the human eye cannot see because the wavelengths are too short. Ultraviolet light from the sun or another source can cause sunburn or even skin cancer.

For More Information

American Academy of Dermatology
P.O. Box 4014
Schaumburg, IL 60168-4014
(847) 330-0230
(888) 462-3376
Web site: http://www.aad.org

National Alopecia Areata Foundation
P.O. Box 150760
San Rafael, CA 94915-0760
(415) 472-3780
e-mail: info@naaf.org
Web site: http://www.naaf.org

National Center for Complementary and Alternative
    Medicine Clearinghouse
National Institutes of Health
P.O. Box 7923
Gaithersburg, MD 20898
(301) 519-3153
(888) 644-6226
e-mail: info@nccam.nih.gov
Web site: http://www.nccam.nih.gov

National Institute of Arthritis and Musculoskeletal and
    Skin Diseases
National Institutes of Health
1 AMS Circle
Bethesda, MD 20892-3675
(301) 495-4484
(877) 226-4267
e-mail: NIAMSInfo@mail.nih.gov
Web site: http://www.niams.nih.gov

Web Sites

Due to the changing nature of Internet links, the Rosen
Publishing Group, Inc., has developed an online list of Web
sites related to the subject of this book. This site is updated
regularly. Please use this link to access the list:

http://www.rosenlinks.com/gdd/alar

For Further Reading

Boudreau, Gloria. *The Immune System*. San Diego, CA: KidHaven Press, 2004.

Bush, Claire. *Modern Day Hairy Tales*. Auckland, New Zealand: Clarity Publishing, 2000.

Fridell, Ron. *Decoding Life: Unraveling the Mysteries of the Genome*. Minneapolis, MN: Lerner Publishing Group, 2004.

Garvy, Helen. *The Immune System: Your Magic Doctor*. Los Gatos, CA: Shire Press, 1992.

Hunt, Nigel, and Sue McHale. *Understanding Alopecia*. London, England: Sheldon Press, 2004.

Krasnow, David, and Lew Parker, eds. *Genetics*. Milwaukee, WI: Gareth Stevens Publishing, 2003.

Mollel, Tololwa M. *The Princess Who Lost Her Hair: An Akamba Legend*. Mahwah, NJ: Troll Communications, 1993.

Murphy-Melas, Elizabeth. *The Girl with No Hair: A Story About Alopecia Areata*. Albuquerque, NM: Health Press, 2003.

Peterseil, Yaacov. *Princess Alopecia*. Jerusalem, Israel: Pitspopany Press, 1999.

Thompson, Wendy, and Jerry Shapiro. *Alopecia Areata: Understanding and Coping with Hair Loss*. Baltimore, MD: Johns Hopkins University Press, 1996.

Bibliography

Aghaei, Shahin. "Topical Immunotherapy of Severe Alopecia Areata with Diphenylcyclopropenone (DPCP): Experience in an Iranian Population." *BMC Dermatology*. Retrieved September 2005 (http://www.biomedcentral.com/1471-5945/5/6).

Bolduc, Chantal, et al. "Alopecia Areata." eMedicine.com. Retrieved September 2005 (http://www.emedicine.com/DERM/topic14.htm).

Freyschmidt-Paul, P. "Therapeutic Trials of Alopecia Areata in C3H/HeJ Mice." 2003 conference of European Hair Research Society. Retrieved September 2005 (http://www.ehrs.org/conferenceabstracts/2003barcelona/guestlectures/L-07-freyschmidt-paul.htm).

Gilhar, Amos. "Acceleration of Organ Restricted Autoimmune Disease by Loss of Immune Privilege: Alopecia Areata Induced in C3H/HeJ Mice by Interferon-Gamma." Orphanet. Retrieved September 2005 (http://orphanet.infobiogen.fr/associations/AAA/AAA17.html).

"International Presence for Skin Disease Groups." *NAAF Newsletter*, Spring 2005.

Judson, Horace F. *The Eighth Day of Creation: Makers of the Revolution in Biology*. Retrieved November 2005 (http://www.fmi.ch/members/marilyn.vaccaro/ewww/eighth.day.creation.htm).

King, Lloyd E., Jr., and John P. Sundberg. "Focus on Research: Alopecia Areata, Or—What's in a Mouse?" *Dermatology Focus*. Retrieved September 2005 (http://dermatologyfoundation.org/pdf/pubs/DF_Winter_2004.pdf).

Lagerkvist, Ulf. *DNA Pioneers and Their Legacy*. Retrieved November 2005 (http://www.fmi.ch/members/marilyn.vaccaro/ewww/dna.pioneer.excerpt.htm).

Lippert-Rasmussen, K. Review of *Gene Therapy and Ethics*, edited by A. Nordgren. *Journal of Medical Ethics*. Retrieved October 2005 (http://jme.bmjjournals.com/cgi/content/full/28/1/58-a).

"NAAF New York Meeting Highlights Two Key Scientific Discoveries." *NAAF Newsletter*, Spring 2005.

"National Alopecia Areata Registry: How You Can Help Researchers Find the Answers." *NAAF Newsletter*, Spring 2005.

National Institute of Arthritis and Musculoskeletal and Skin Diseases. "National Registry Established for Alopecia Areata." Press release. Retrieved October 2005 (http://www.niams.nih.gov/ne/press/2001/02_20.htm).

Pericin, M., and R. M. Trüeb. "Topical Immunotherapy of Severe Alopecia Areata with Diphenylcyclopropenone: Evaluation of 68 Cases." *Dermatology*. Retrieved September 2005 (http://content.karger.com/ProdukteDB/produkte.asp?Aktion=ShowPDF&ProduktNr=224164&Ausgabe=225575&ArtikelNr=17935&filename=17935.pdf).

Price, Vera H. "Therapy of Alopecia Areata: On the Cusp and in the Future." *Journal of Investigative Dermatology Symposium Proceedings*. Retrieved September 2005 (http://www.blackwell-synergy.com/doi/abs/10.1046/j.1087-0024.2003.00811.x).

Rubenstein, Irwin. "DNA." *World Book Multimedia Encyclopedia*. Chicago, IL: World Book, 2002.

Rubenstein, Irwin, and Susan M. Wick. "Cell." *World Book Multimedia Encyclopedia.* Chicago, IL: World Book, 2002.

Skurkovich, B., and S. Skurkovich. "Anti-Interferon-Gamma Antibodies in the Treatment of Autoimmune Diseases." *Current Opinion in Molecular Therapeutics.* Retrieved October 2005 (http://www.ncbi.nlm.nih.gov/entrez/query.fcgi?cmd= Retrieve&db=PubMed&list_uids=12669471&dopt=Abstract).

Steinbrecher, Ricarda. "What Is Genetic Engineering?" *Synthesis/Regeneration: A Magazine of Green Social Thought.* Retrieved October 2005 (http://online.sfsu.edu/ %7Erone/GEessays/WhatisGE.html).

Sundberg, John P., and Lloyd E. King Jr. "Mouse Alopecia Areata Models: An Array of Data on Mechanisms and Genetics." *Journal of Investigative Dermatology Symposium Proceedings.* Retrieved September 2005 (http://www.blackwell-synergy.com/doi/abs/10.1046/ j.1087-0024.2003.00804.x).

Thiedke, C. Carolyn. "Alopecia in Women." *American Family Physician.* Retrieved November 2005 (http:// www.aafp.org/afp/20030301/1007.html).

Thompson, Wendy, and Jerry Shapiro. *Alopecia Areata: Understanding and Coping with Hair Loss.* Baltimore, MD: Johns Hopkins University Press, 1996.

Tobin, D. J., S. H. Gardner, P. B. Luther, S. M. Dunston, N. J. Lindsey, and T. Olivry. "A Natural Canine Homologue of Alopecia Areata in Humans." *British Journal of Dermatology.* Retrieved September 2005 (http:// www.medscape.com/viewarticle/465486).

"What We Have Learned in the Past Five Years." *NAAF Newsletter,* Fall 2005.

"What We Learned in the 1980s." *NAAF Newsletter,* Fall 2005.

"What We Learned in the 1990s." *NAAF Newsletter,* Fall 2005.

Index

About the Author

Janey Levy is a writer and editor living in Colden, New York. The author of more than fifty books for young people, she has written extensively for the Rosen Publishing Group's class-room division. She has an interest in autoimmune diseases because she suffers from one known as fibromyalgia. Levy has a PhD from the University of Kansas.

Photo Credits

Cover top © Eye of Science/Photo Researchers, Inc.; cover inset, p. 1 © www.istockphoto.com/Arnold van Rooij; cover back-ground images: © www.istockphoto.com/Rafal Zdeb (front right), © Jim Wehtje/Photodisc/PunchStock (front middle), © www.istockphoto.com (back middle, back right), © Lawrence Lawry/Photodisc/PunchStock (back left); p. 5 © Logical Images/Custom Medical Stock Photo, Inc.; p. 8 © Martin Hemmington, National Fox Welfare Society; p. 9 © Mary Evans Picture Library/Alamy; p. 13 © BSIP, Gilles/Science Photo Library; p. 17 © Bettmann/Corbis; p. 18 U.S. Department of Energy Human Genome Program, www.ornl.gov/hgmis; p. 19 © Courtesy of the Tennessee State Library and Archives; p. 20 © Courtesy of the National Institutes of Health; p. 22 © Yoav Levy/Phototake, Inc./Alamy; p. 27 © ISM/Phototake, Inc.; p. 28 © Mediscan/Medical-on-Line/Alamy; p. 29 © AP/Wide World Photos/Bob Child; p. 30 © BSIP, Chassenet/Science Photo Library; p. 32 © Phanie/Photo Researchers, Inc.; p. 34 www.naaf.org/kids/teen-wear.asp; p. 37 Kathleen A. Silva/Dr. John P. Sundberg, courtesy of the Jackson Laboratory; p. 40 © Frances M. Roberts/Getty Images; p. 42 © Dr. P. Marazzi/Science Photo Library; p. 45 © Michel Gilles/Photo Researchers, Inc.; p. 49 © Carol Donner/Phototake, Inc./Alamy; p. 50 © AP/Wide World Photos/Moscow Pullman Daily News, Geoff Crimmins.

Designer: Evelyn Horovicz; Editor: Christopher Roberts